THE
TEXTING
GAME

THE
TEXTING
GAME

PART II

DOREMUS YOUNG

THE TEXTING GAME
PART II

iUniverse books may be ordered through booksellers or by contacting:

iUniverse
1663 Liberty Drive
Bloomington, IN 47403
www.iuniverse.com
1-800-Authors (1-800-288-4677)

ISBN: 978-1-6632-0441-7 (sc)
ISBN: 978-1-6632-0442-4 (e)

Print information available on the last page.

iUniverse rev. date: 07/28/2020

I

Part two was right around Super bowl time; well the playoffs had just ended. The New Orleans Saints and Indianapolis Colts were the leagues two most competitive dominating teams. Everyone in the texting game of part one is pretty much in part two and maybe some more players except maybe they didn't return any messages. So, let's just say they fell off not dispersing gold mail in the game.

You had to decide who won in part one because part two is a little more intense. Some people don't like texting or they just don't like the person texting them. I can understand that because you aren't the only one with a humbugging text buddy.

I believe I was still working at Pizza Inn at the time… "Goodnight" [received from: Janez @ 1:06:33 am February 4, 2010]. "Loll. I was texting you. You don't text me back" [Received from: Lil Bit @ 1:53:56am].

"Last night when you text me I text you back and besides I don't ever know when you are at work or busy" [Received from: Lil Bit@ 1:59:20 am]. "Goodnight" [Received from: Janez @ 12:37:14am February 5, 2010]. "Let's go for New Orleans! But, I got my money on the Colts! I want to watch the Super bowl with you [Sent to: Lil Bit @ 4:25:25pm February 6, 2010]. I don't care if you don't watch football? (Emoticon sunglasses) Let's get some pizza and hot wings and we can drink whatever" [Sent to: Lil Bit @ 4:35:11pm]. "I thought we were going to talk" [Sent to: Black @ 5:09:48pm]. "No. I'm just now getting off work. I guess you ready to stop this texting" [Received from Lil Bit @ 2:38:15 am February 7]? "Loll. I don't even know who's playing in the Super bowl. Loll" [Received from Lil Bit @ 5:17:05pm] "I'm calling you soon as I get

1

some minutes, all right" [Sent to Lil Bit @ 5:25: 55pm]? "Okay well, I'm not into football like that, loll I'm going to New Orleans the 16th for Fat Tuesday" [Received from Lil Bit @ 5:27:01pm].

I believe I was still working at Pizza Inn at the time. However, these are random messages to let you know who is still in the game. I never really worked enough hours to complain about how tired I was. So, getting in the bed early was out of the question. I used to find a reason just to stay awake, like smoking weed, afraid that I would miss something going on during regular people lives. Everything kind of kicks off in the AM... Late midnight, we talked. Early daybreak, we talked. We talked during the best sleeping hours. "You sleep baby?" I asked Lil Bit. I don't know what she's doing up this late. Hell! I don't know why I'm still up, but shocking, but true, she replied in approximately one hour and three minutes, "Halfway there. "What's up?" That was indicator that she was already in bed. Just as if I was right by her side, I'm trying to cuddle and get in that ear until we both fall asleep. I did just that. I fell asleep and she fell asleep, but she went to sleep right after her first text. Me, I continued texting up until 4:25:05 am talking about dam football. "We still on for tomorrow" [Sent to Lil Bit @ 4:10:17am]? Matter or fact, the next six messages are sent to Lil Bit. "You know its Super bowl" (Emoticon: smiling sunglasses) [Sent to Lil Bit @ 4:25:05 am]?

"What's up Lil ma? Are you going to church [Sent @ 12:03pm February 8, 2010]?

Don't just leave me texting you. "That isn't for laughing out loud (loll) [Sent@12:13:34pm]! Get your phat ass up then, and call me" [Sent @ 12:24:35 pm! "I'm still sleeping." She finally replied @ 1:21:20pm

At least I knew she read my messages. Maybe she just rolled over and finally noticed the phone ringing, beeping, or whatever it does. Now that I got your attention, I can let you know how I feel. "Now bang." "I know you wanted to chill, but I am just going to work tonight. "I am going to make it up to you. "Ok?" It's now 3:35:02pm, and stills no reply. I done became impatient, "It is now 4:31:44pm so I ask, "you gone sleep all day?" She finally respond at 4:57:43pm, "I been sleep allay." I thought... True. That wasn't even a smart remark, now that I think about it. I can say it took all day for this conversation to start, but it didn't last near the length of time she slept. "You must have heard something bad about me?" I must have gotten worried or something and don't know why. "What's up?" [Sent @ 5:21: pm] You don't get points unless you score. I scored because I got game. "Call you back in a second." She replied [sent @ 5:32:26pm]. There were no more messages this day.

The next day, Janez sends a shocking message, a rather serious message, a message I thought I would send her. "Hello stranger." She said. "I have not heard from you in a while. "You must have found another friend?" It kind of shocked me, but I smiled like "somebody". Plus I had a legitimate comeback. "Now what make you say something like that? I asked. Nope. I continued, "I just got off work" [Sent @ 11:52: pm].

Every message is sent and returned at any given time, but you want need an exact time for every message, maybe frequently, but definitely a new date every day.

II

Of course, Lil Bit and I talked periodically, but I guess wishfully thinking for anything extra is always an extra wish. It would be late anytime I called or text. When I say late, I mean later that midnight. It would just be spare moments when I realize everybody else is either sleep or have cut their phone off for the night just so it would fully charge. Oh, the phone boning doesn't stop. I can phone bone if I can't… if you want…– let's just get back to the game. It's just like setting picks, throwing strikes, making the right block, or simply knowing your position. The only difference in texting is when and where or time and location.

Like baseball, every pitch is not meant to be a strike because you might be a homerun hitter up to bat who is lured to pitch a fastball to. See, the thing about baseball, you don't get a chance to score right after I get an RBI, hit a homerun, or just steal a base. You get a chance to stop me from scoring.

In Basketball, you don't have to set picks or screens every time you run up and down the court. It's really not necessary especially if you're out of position, but you can score right after. You can also prevent me from scoring by defending one side of the court. It's called keeping the ball in your court or possession. Football is a little bit different because you have to be a blocker the whole game whether you are a lineman, running back, or wide receiver. It's the same with scoring just like basketball.

Sending text messages could get you shut-down if you send the wrong thing. You can even lose a contact. Then, you have no game. I like to stay in it while I'm winning.

"It's raining outside… I informed Lil Bit. "You should be talking so good to me right now." I continued. It's 2:19:02am, sending this non returned message to Lil Bit February 9, 2010. There was no reply in less than ten minutes so I got worried, "you okay?" I asked fearfully. I figure since you work late nights, then possibly you'll be awake after hours. Nope, that will not happen in this day and time. I didn't hear from her in about two or three days.

Now when I talk to Janez it's usually on the weekend, early in the morning, or anytime. Flexibility around your schedule is the key to this game. Later that morning I woke up with something on my mind. With her, she knows exactly what it is. "What up bay?" I greet her. I got my mind made up now referring to question about finding another friend. "I want you and honesty I can't have you right now. I remember that she is a little younger than me. So I ask, "Who's going to be strong? "You for me or me for you (loll)" [Sent @ 9:52:23 am]? Janez doesn't text me right back either. Really, no one does unless their eager or very worse. About five minutes to twelve noon she text back. "We can be strong for each other." She replied. And that is how a message should be returned only if the two are serious.

For some people this time of the year is back to school time. It's time to lick the ham, flush the chitterlings, and put Christmas away until winter. However, this next Christmas Janez has an eighteenth birthday. She is legal. In other words Janez has fully matured into a natural grown woman. It's hard to wait on somebody in this life, but somewhere in America everybody is patiently waiting on somebody; the significant other.

I would sometimes talk to Janez throughout the whole day. We would talk in the morning, sometimes, noon, and at night. Later that night I was just thinking about my girl/woman. "Chillin… I let her know what I'm doing. "I want to call you, but I'm watching movies." I said. Are you alright?" I had to make sure she knew.

She had to be busy doing school work or basically getting prepared for the next day like regular working people. Because about an hour later she text me, "Hey friend. "What are you doing?" She asked. I didn't reply, so about ten minutes later Janez text right back. "Call me a little later on."

We must have talked later that night before bed because I didn't text her back until February 12, 2010. She didn't text me until Valentine's Day.

I remember being in Downtown Collins at Wards Restaurant when I received a surprise message from Lil Bit. I couldn't believe that she actually text me first. "This is Lil Bit. "This is my new number (with a signature reading *2Hot 2Handle*)." She said. [Received from Lil Bit @ 1:10:30pm February 12, 2010] I didn't text back. So, around 5pm she text back, "Call you later ([*2Hot2Handle])."

Maybe I went to work that night because my phone didn't receive any messages. I know for sure I sent a text to Janez when I got off because she is getting ready for the 2010 Basketball Playoffs for Perry Central High School. "What's up bay? "I forgot you were getting ready for playoffs. "Loll. "Let me know how your game goes. "I guessing you will hit about 5 free throws, 2 blocks, and a steal just for me... (Loll)" I continued. I always tease her about her game but its only encouragement for the team.

Valentine's Day finally arrived and I got 'buku love'. Janez was the first to text. She sent, "HAPPY VALENTINES DAY!" She did this before noon. Tiffany, my sister sent the same message about 10 minutes later, "HAPPY VALENTINES DAY!" After that matter I wished everybody Happy Valentines in a group message. No body replied at the same time, but I received a message from: Black saying, "Same to you [@ 11:36:54am], a University of Southern Mississippi Graduate student named Angel who I had recently met saying, "Thank you [@11:38:02am], even somebody who doesn't recognize my number replied; "who is this" [@ 12:12:21pm]? I sent text back, "Dra" [12:15:00pm]. I was hoping the name would help remember. My mom even replied, "Thank you baby and the same to you" [@12:39:37]. All of the greetings were received within one hour, so you know that makes you feel like somebody anyway.

Valentine's Day had come and gone and everything was getting back to normal. No more holidays. No more breaks. Now it's back to the business. The next big event would be Super bowl, but it's always on Sunday. That's kind of big for a good weekend. Maybe a week had passed since Valentine's Day. I'm sure I talked some on the phone, but no gold mail. Maybe this is a two week work week and I worked 3 or 4 days. However, everybody needs a break. "Hey buddy. "What you up to" Asked Janez [February 20 @ 9:15:09]? There was no reply. Maybe I called and talked after receiving message. The next day, well midnight, my brother wanted to know if I was going to the club. "You were going to the club?" Asked Maurice[@ 12:17:46 am on 2-21-10]. There was no reply. Maybe I went to the club that night.

You know when you feel bored for being at home so long or when you just get off work? February 23, 2010 I must have worked from 4pm-10pm. During work I had to think about how I can make this person call. I have been flipping pizzas and it is not that bad. I had been thinking about Lil Bit. Its 11:46:49pm and she had not sent a text or called. I'm always forgetting her working late hours. "Loll!" I sent text.

It seems like she only text me when I text her, but when she responds to me It seems like she's been waiting for me to break the ice. "What is up? "It seems like you forgot how to use your charm, breaking the ice. "Have you found a new friend" [sent to Lil Bit @ 12:16:05 am February 25, 2010]? I remember talking on the phone with her one weekend. She told me she was going to the coast and hung up the phone. Since I didn't get a reply from the last message and I don't know how or what you did on the coast; you got to tell me something. "Damn. I uttered. Did you ever make it from the coast? I haven't heard from you since the night you went to the casino. What is going on (emoticon angry frustration)?" I asked. "Loll." She replied [@12:37:51am]. "Oh you still got that charm on me loll. I stated. I just don't get you. You look nice and sweet to me, but you want to play hard to get. I grunted. Why?" I asked [12:55:17am]. Well between midnight hours and that day we didn't resume talking. We talked later that night. So, life goes on.

III

Lil Bit and I had begun to text more and more. She told me this is what she does by the way. Our conversations had become mature and natural. For some reason I felt this would bring us to some type of relationship or at least relations. When I message someone, it's usually a follow up from the last message unless change is necessary. In this chapter you might not get a stated time for every message. Just know that each conversation is a technical message sent through and or received through via telephone screen. I rather read like it's a script or novel. "Is believe spelled "ie" or "ei" (loll)? I asked Lil Bit. "I'm serious. I forgot how to spell." I mentioned. She sent her text, "Lmao". She replied. "See, you think shit funny. I'm for real." I confessed. "It's like I led you with my first impression, now I must wait for you to impress me." I declared. "If you would have told me how to spell a simple word, I would have been impressed." "Loll. You didn't ask me to spell nothing big-head." She replies. "See ignorant shit like that start arguments." I retorted. "You are crazy! "You are crazy!" She repeated.

I went to work the next day but my cell phone had been turned off. Evidently, I didn't pay my bill. I had to use the company's phone at Pizza Inn. I called my brother because I hadn't quite learned Daddy's number by heart. It was 11:41:25pm and I was ready to go, "Call Daddy. I suggested. Tell him I'm off and need a ride to the crib. I don't have any minutes. I indicated. Call Pizza Inn and let me know something."

I had enough text messages to send. In fact that's what my phone plan consist of. I had nothing but text messages, probably five dollars for 500 messages. Yep, that was the phone plan, the Go Phone. They even had a plan for a payment of $9.99 for 1,000 text messages. I always thought 1,000 messages were impossible to send, so I just stick with the 500 plan. I don't remember what time I made it home, but dad would usually be on time. Also, I don't remember if this was a leap year or just 28 days this month, but no one text me for about a week. I guess I didn't want to be bothered. I really wanted to see how soon anyone changed their number or allow their phone to be disconnected. That is very tempting but, nobody cares. "What do you do when your phone ring? I asked Lil Bit... What's up?" I beckoned ([sent 3-04-10 @ 1:34:23 pm)]. "Hit the ignore button." She indicates. "Do you have to run from me?" I assumed. I didn't get a text nor reply for about 8 hours. By the 11 o'clock hour, I couldn't take it. I got frustrated and felt ignored. "Alright, I spoke. You answered my question, but I don't ever give you the silent treatment." I continued loll! "I did not. She said. I am busy when you call me. Plus I be at work and I be working hard sweetie." She exclaimed ((([*Sexy-Red*)].

That's ok I thought, but "I would hate for you not to be busy at work. They cannot have you working so hard that you can't make time for yourself baby." I argued. "You said, for my what?" She yelled [(*Sexy-Red*)]. Perhaps she didn't understand what I said. "I hate how you just pretend you don't know what I'm talking about. I elaborated. I said they don't have to make it seem like you don't have time for yourself!" I repeated.

Well, another day had passed and it was midnight again. I barely talk on the phone because for some reason I don't like to talk for long hours. Its March 5, 2010 2:21:51 am. I must be a stalker and didn't know it, but Lil Bit is consistent returning my messages. I believe some of the shit I say is made pointless. Others may say the same.

Since every action has a reaction, then act on this, "You up for talking tonight? I asked. "Lol. I'm not going to call if you're not. I'm just texting you, so text me too." I demanded. "We can text. "I'm too tired to talk on the phone. She replied convincingly. That was her last message for the midnight hours. I continued texting just to get the last word. "Ok I know you got plans. I rambled as if I was Smokey in the movie Friday. "First, let me be involved. I think it's more to you than just trust. Second, I know you work hard and it probably pays off; I don't know. Third, look how I reach out to you through these messages." (Lol) I think I torcher her.

I think I'm on the verge of running this girl off by a text message. I don't know if everybody think about what they send before they send it, but "common since" was written by Thomas Payne. He was not a factor in the game. These messages are written by me and the replier or whomever it may concern.

Whatever I do during the morning is probably sleeping or thinking, but receiving gold mail was definitely a priority throughout the rest of the day. Any message that you can send I could reply. Don't get me wrong, texting is not for everybody. It makes you wonder, who thinks like this when you are actually speaking? Who talks like this when you are actually listening? I do. "I'm trying to figure a way to break the ice with you. I encouraged Lil Bit. It's almost like I'm in competition with someone else... Spell impossible." I teased [@ 2:53:56 pm]. No matter what I say, she would say whatever is on her mind and it made it make since. "You are weird to me." She replied ([*Sexy-Red*)]. Then we carried on. "What is weird about me and not weird about you?" I asked vaguely. "A lot is weird about you. She answered. Even though that's you, you can stop texting my phone sir because we aren't ever going to make nothing happen. I don't want to keep wasting your time." She continued.

For some reason I don't think she likes me anymore. It is becoming a joke or just fun and games. "You are not wasting my time. I insisted. I am a person you could really talk to." I convinced. At 4:48:01 pm I convinced her that we should be friends. "Could we be friends?" I asked. I also smiled as well as laugh out loud (emoticon with happy smiling face)! Ten minutes later she text back ok like everything cool again.

IV

Since we're in the month of March, fraternities and sororities are having their traditional Q-Delta weekend festivities. I'm not an actual member, but everybody is welcomed to join or attend all events. Everything that brings a crowd happens during Q-Delta. Concerts, Talent shows, standup comedy, Step shows, Barbeques, Meets and Greet, Competition are all part of fun filled weekend, etc. I didn't get the pleasure to show up for this weekend. I was probably undecided because I knew the fun was worth more money than I had. Anyway, I worked. "Are you going to Q-Delta? I asked Lil Bit [@ 4:54:02 pm 3-5-10]. I have to work because everybody requested the day off." I continued. "Yeah I'm going. She answered. "You're not coming to the club?" She asked ([*Sexy-Red*]).

I like how Lil Bit keeps the conversation normal. Since we're only reading each other contemplated thoughts, but a complete sentence help when you follow up with the same topic, "You aint coming to the club?" Lil Bit asked. I couldn't give her a direct answer, so like anybody would do, I give excuses. "I don't know. I responded. I'm cleaning up the house right now." I continued. "I'm talking about tomorrow night. She insisted. "You got to work too?" Asked Lil Bit ([*Sexy-Red*]) (@ 5:08pm). "Yes." I answered [@ 5:27:28pm].

Later that night I heard a popular rap group would perform at the Multi- Purpose Center in Hattiesburg. I added a couple more recipients to this message. I wanted to know who really going to give me gold mail. I sent the same message to Lil Bit, my ex-special friend Crystal G and my soon to be ole lady, Janez. "Drake is in the building with Young Money tonight." I informed Lil Bit [@10:43:08 pm] "Drake is in the building with Young Money tonight." I informed Crystal [@ 10:43:30 pm].

There was no reply from the two recipients so I indirectly asked Janez if she was going out. "You are going to see Young Money and Drake tonight?" I ramblingly asked [@ 10: 46:28 pm]. "No I'm not going." She replied [@ 10:47: 03 pm]. March 5, 2010 had ended.

She didn't have to, but Mom text me all the way from Chattanooga, TN saying, "Hey baby. Momma said. All is well. She elaborated. "Love and miss ya. She continued. "Tiffany and Mom are here and we are eating" Mom informed [3-6-10 @ 5:08: 07]. At the time I was at work at Pizza Inn. Some jobs you got it made when your phone rings because you could take at least a minute before you start production and answer. "What's up? I replied. "I love you all. "I'm getting ready to go flip pizza (Loll)". I explained. I remember having braids/ plaits in my head before my little cousin Ashley snatched one of my plaits off of my head attempting to take the plait and untangle it. "I got a bald head (emoticon smiley face with shades) [@5:13:02 pm]." I told momma. Mom was shocked. About an hour later she wanted to make sure of what I said. "You got a what?" She asked curiously. "I have a bald head (emoticon half smiling with shades)." I responded with confidence. "Are you for real? She continued. (Lol), I bet you look handsome with it!" She complemented.

Yep. I had to rock a bald head because my little cousin had snatched a bald spot in the top of my head right above my forehead. I used my Dads hair clippers. First, I took some scissors and clipped the remaining plaits. Then I resumed with my hair cut. It felt funny, but it didn't look that bad. I was just a new face with an old bald head or should I say "ole head?"

V

I got off work late that night. It was about thirty minutes past twelve. Since I didn't have my own transportation I had to catch rides home. Some nights I would work with my brother or my Step Mother. On these nights I would work till closing time. I worked with different shift leaders on the nights scheduled to work. I worked with another shift leader tonight so I need a ride home. My brother Maurice stayed awake until I made it home. I rode home with my stepmother and we rode through a road block. I warned my brother, "road blocks in Covington County Collins" [@ 1:39:17 am 3-07-10]. After that I thought to myself, Lil Bit hadn't called or text. She never really calls, but she didn't send me any gold mail for about two days, which makes me mad. If I was to solicit women for the gain of money then that would make me a pimp. Good thing I'm not because I would be two days behind getting paid. Instead I solicit grammar for the receipt or gain of gold mail.

Gold mail is a pop up icon desktop feature indicating a new message. Depending on the type of phone you owned, recipients probably didn't get gold mail. Like a hustler chases money, I'm chasing gold mail. I finally made it home barely 2:00 in the morning. To my surprise I didn't get any gold mail on the 7th. It doesn't bother me when I don't because I know I can get mail. I can get mail or entertainment. Lil Bit just became entertained with my persistence because I didn't know her and I wasn't scared to take the challenge to get to either. "What's up sexy? I greeted [1:53:18am]. "What you Looking (emoticons licking out its tongue substituting letter o's) like (lol)! I was curiously asking. Send your boy a picture or something..." I must have thought she was easy and would send me at least a half-naked picture of her in lingerie some booty shorts or something… However, that wasn't the case and I went to sleep without a picture or any gold mail.

Sleeping without the extra incentives wasn't that bad. Of course I didn't lose any sleep, but I was losing control of how and when to text. I don't start fights. I start conversation. The next morning I don't recall exactly the time it was when I awake. I imagine it had to be early because my brother Cozart was back in town and we went riding towards the Magee area.

It had to be about noon when I realized that we were kind of in her neighborhood, but I don't know exactly where she lives so at 11:52: am I let her know, "What up friend? I got my brother with me and we are about to head your way so, get-up mane and let a brother come through… "Is that cool?" I asked. Time passed. As a matter of the fact, a few hours had passed. Evidently we ate our own breakfast, lunch and made it back on our side in that length of time. She still didn't call back. "We have left and you didn't call back (emoticon smiley with shades) [@ 4:53: pm]. I retorted. I went to work afterwards, but my dad didn't know, so I let Maurice know, "What up? Call daddy. Tell him I work at 5." I said [5:39:01 pm]. I gave him about ten minutes to call and then I double checked to make sure, "You call? What did he say?" I asked. Not a minute later, he replied, "Yeah." So, not only did I have a whole day anticipating seeing Lil Bit, but I had a ride to and from work with no problem.

Maurice must have been in Collins the whole day. Either that or he was ready to go to the "Burg". "Are you off work yet?" He asked [@ 12:36:00 am 3-08-10]. Assuming he was ready to ride I just told him, I'm in the house for tonight (emoticon smiley with glasses) [@ 1:09:25 am]. Besides, Dad picked me up from work early before 12. "That's alright bro." He replied [1:10:43]. Dad usually has a couple of beers waiting for me when I get home. But, I always had a blunt to go with the beer. He would tell me, "You could take these couple of beers in your room and chill." But, I would sometimes drink them outside and listen to the radio in his truck.

VI

Even though I didn't see Lil Bit yesterday, I didn't stop playing the game. Nowadays it's hard to lose friends because of MySpace, Facebook, and all the different chat-lines. Back in the days you could accidentally dial the wrong number and there would usually be a 7 out of 10 chance that you might develop a small conversation which would lead to meeting a new friend. The disadvantage to meeting somebody dialing the wrong number is you don't know who or what they look like. She may sound good when you call and that keeps you talking. The first time you meet may be the last time you call or get a phone call. Before you meet you may talk for a week just to find out the main interest there is to know in a person. It's really an approach to anybody that you meet face to face. I call this the "Don't Look, just Talk Approach". I used this approach on Lil Bit. I like this approach because it has become useless to keep trying to see her. The game must go on. One reason, if I lose I'm not a sore loser, but it doesn't mean I play to lose either. Later that night I used "Don't Look, just Talk Approach".

"A, what year did you graduate from high school?" I asked [@10:37:24 3-8-10]. Before I continue, I know you're thinking. Why haven't you been asked this question? One reason is I'm 10 years out of high school and so is she. Another reason is common since because we're like the same age. However, I did get a reply. I didn't get it right away nor did I get an answer. Better yet I skipped that question and figured maybe that's dumb to ask. So, "did you have a goodtime over the weekend (emoticon nervous expression)?" I added. There still was no reply. "Home girl, I should have met you on MySpace, we probably could have been the best of friends.

Lol" I teased her with the tone [@11:13:16pm]. I just put the phone down since it took all that. As soon as I put it down the ringtone I just downloaded, "Why you thug me like that" by Lil Boosie went buzzing flashing gold mail. (Why you thug me like that? I don't know. I don't mean to. Sometimes I feel like I don't need you."(Lil Boosie). Instead of grabbing the phone with excitement, I just laid back and listened to my [ringtone singing along as if the radio was on. She finally replied [@11:14:19] with the signature [*Sexy-Red*] when I finally checked my mail. Now that my line is in the water, I think I'm on to something. Instead of being bored the whole hour of eleven o'clock, we texted. "You are silly." She said. I sent her a reply, but I didn't say anything. I sent a blank message to tease her thinking maybe this will give you a clue of what the hell I go through when I randomly text you anything at all. "Why did you send me a blank text? "You are crazy. [*Sexy-Red*]" She noted. "Yeah I did, but I'm not crazy (emoticon smiling with a smirk)" I answered. "Yes you are crazy [*Sexy-Red*]. She reiterated.

As you can see, I just created a small argument, but please let us finish? "I must be crazy to let you get inside my head (emoticon mug looking crazy)." I said. "Lol. "How could I get inside your head? [*Sexy-Red*]" Asked Lil Bit. Before I answer her I'm going to tell her about herself. "Just because you're slow (emoticon shocked expression) doesn't mean you have to avoid your friends, friend (lol)" [11:59:26: pm 3-08-10]. I still didn't answer her question. "Shut up! "You're slow your damn self [Sexy-Red*]" She replied [12:14:08 am 3-9-10] "That's what took you so long to recognize my doggish ways (emoticon smirk smiley with shades)?" I taunted her aggravation. "Stop texting me [*Sexy-Red*]." She warned [@1:32:29 am]. I must have really pissed her off or she was just fed up with the bullshit. Nonetheless, the game is getting very intense and everybody who is playing is hitting on all cylinders. I can't stop now. "You getting mad can't take a joke! "I'll holler at you. "Peace (lol)!" I told her.

I wasn't mad, like angry mad, but I was mad like aggravated mad. So, I figured I'm just going to have a little fun. It didn't bother me enough to dwell on. It's like freestyle or prep high school wrestling. If your opponent takes you down on the mat, you give up what is called "Take down points". This doesn't necessarily mean that the match is finished. It means you have to get back in the game and go hard, get back in control. More or less, defeat your opponent. I really had to get her off my mind and out of my head just for a moment or enough time to regroup. "You still up (emoticon smiley with smart glasses)?" I asked Janez [@1:54:28]. I knew she was in the bed because she's a junior in high school ready to get that shit over with.

Now, must I remind you? I did not work a third shift job. I did not work a first shift job. I barely worked second shift. Let's just say part-time allowed me to get my game on all shifts. "You should be off work by now. I alarmed Lil Bit. "Call me before you get home. I told her. "Okay? [2:28:58am]" I didn't get a reply. I don't think I even got an answer when I called her. I did the same thing anybody else would do with the free time I had. I stayed up. Since it was so late in the morning or should I say late in the night; better yet dusk before dawn, I wanted to try and mellow things out, "Real shit. "Why do you want to stunt on me (lol)?" I asked solemnly [@4:05:20 am]. For sure she didn't actually get this message when I sent it. It was 4:00 in the morning for heaven's sake. I went to bed after that and woke up about noon only to crank this mother-fucking game up. I thank you Jesus for waking us (me) up this morning. That's a short prayer I use to get my day started.

VII

I wake up on days like this and basically you just follow up on the day before. What I mean by follow up is carry out the day with the important things you started yesterday. It's obvious that 24 hours is not enough time to do all there need to be done for anonymous occasions. 24 hours is enough time to do what you have to do considering time management and proper preparation. Procrastination and cramming will... Let's just get back to the game.

Since Janez is in school and I didn't get a wakeup call from Lil Bit no one is really defending their game. All left to do when one is tired or can't play is what? That is right. You relieve them and never give up. There is always time for improvement; even in 24 hours.

I love waking up talking to the person who is willing to wait the game out. Texting isn't really a game. It's not a physical game. It is mental. However it is serious because like any other game, it has its precautions. You may be familiar with the slogan "Don't Text and Drive". This is very serious. You can compare some of the rules and regulations from any sport on your own time. Right now I have a game to play. Like halftime shows and intermissions for playwrights; you better grab some popcorn, chips and drinks. If you fall asleep while reading, then follow up.

I know that Janez is in school, but I text her occasionally during the day just for cool points. You can get cool points when you are a "Cool Guy". "What up bay? Don't get into no trouble today" [@1:46:01 pm 3-09-10] lol. I really didn't expect too many replies from Janez because of the age difference. We can only say so much. Everybody else is like comrades and friends, parents or associates, brothers or cousins, freaks and geeks. You can't forget your co-workers. You get the picture.

"What up ape nuts!" Lol. I alarmed Brit Brit [@1:5:05pm]. She soon text back minutes later. "Who is this?" "You act so fucking corny. I replied. "You know who I am by now. I said. "Are you slow?" I continued [1:59:41: pm]. "Who is this? She asked again. "I don't know who you are. She followed. "Who are you?" She screamed.

Right now I'm the kick ball, tennis ball or the ping pong ball. It seems that I keep ending up in someone else's corner. Brit-Brit has really pissed me off because she pretends that she doesn't know who I am. This is enough power to send me back to Lil Bits corner. It is now two in the afternoon and I figure she's still sleep. But wait... Brit-Brit still wants to play the ignorant curiosity game. You know the thriller scary movies Scary Movie"; someone calls and you know who it is, but it will kill you if you don't find out for sure. "Just tell me who you are or stop texting me. She demands. "Who is this?" She asked again. I guess she never did get the text she wanted.

"Wake up! "Wake up! "Wake up!" I alarmed Lil Bit [2:13:39pm]. (Let me digress for a minute. When I attended college back in 2001, spring 2002 remember this was when I was on the road to stardom. To make a long story short; I remember Special Friends Kesha P and Crystal G (in college as well) would call me early before my classes start with the same wakeup call; Wake up! Wake up! Wake up! We had land lines I was late getting a cellular phone back then. Plus I stayed on University of Southern Mississippi campus on the 4th floor in Osceola McCarty Hall. There was no caller Id for me, only a telephone ring and my answer. I'm really not the type to ignore phone calls unless there is caller Id. I would answer the phone and to my surprise the first word I remember is 'wake up'. I heard these words repeatedly three times in a row. Before I could say anything I would slam the phone down on the bed like I do the alarm clock. I miss these good ole days)... She let me text her for a whole hour before she replied. Maybe she was still asleep or just good at her game. At least she didn't get all of my game time for the rest of the day. However, I was just one hell of a player. "Do you know my name? I asked Lil Bit. "Tell the truth. "I think you do" [2:27:14pm]... There was no reply. "Look. "Be a smart-ass if you want. This is very imperative. "I am not scared of you. "Parents just don't understand." I felt like the Fresh Prince of Bel Air. The only difference is it wasn't a joke. [@2:45:14pm] "Why don't you call for five minutes? This is all I ask; five minutes of your precious time. "Is this too much to ask" [3:02:38 pm]? I started to sound like exhaustion as sweat drips from a running athlete whose initial position is at rest standing over a puddle of water, begging for more chances. If this isn't tired, then I don't know what tired is.

As the three o'clock hour hit, she finally gave me what I wanted and it was the same thing she said before. This time it was more sincere, "I have asked you nicely to stop texting my phone. I don't want to talk to you. I want you to leave me alone. Okay" (Sexy-Red)[3:14:42pm]?

This game has gone way out of hand and I can't stand the sight of me losing… But, I want my gold mail. We had a new waitress to join us at Pizza Inn early last month. It took me a little time to get to know her. Plus she was a little more attractive than the others. Plus she would graduate this coming may with all the other high school graduates. Not all of the workers were in high school. Some had graduated last year, attended college, or had kids… In other words, we are all adults in this game. So, drop your pride, but keep your dignity. "What up? Do you work today?" I asked Allison. Allison is part African, part Philippine. I didn't get that much gold mail from her, but she's cool anyway. There was no reply. In fact, I received no gold mail for the rest of the day. It doesn't mean that I stop when the mail stop. I progress.

I acknowledged Lil Bit's request to stop texting her phone, but it was kind of funny because it seems like she got mad at my intention to text. Everybody gets mad at some point. It doesn't matter if you are the coolest person on earth. It doesn't matter if you are the nicest person in a group. Somehow, some way anger management has no control once you release your frustration. In order to avoid conflict, you have to be able to channel your energy in a positive direction.

When I was younger, in my younger days, my little sister use- to-do what we call copy-cat. If this doesn't piss you off, then I don't know what will. However, my intentions were not intended to piss-off Lil Bit. Instead of her being the guilty culprit I am the one with the conflict.

All is left to do is maintain texting. I called and called only to hear (automated systems) that all calls are forwarded to voicemail at this time. The question arises to the reader; who is mad? Is it me or you?

I really don't know a comeback line for anyone telling you to stop texting especially if you are given a warning. Lil Bit did warn me. She told me twice not to text her phone. I accepted her request, but I didn't like her reason. I don't even think she had a reason. "I have asked you nicely to stop texting my phone. I don't want to talk to you. I want you to leave me alone. Okay" [3:19:13pm]?" I forwarded the message back to her. One minute later I let her know I wasn't mad, that I didn't even care. "Cool (emoticon smiley with shades). See you on the town. Bye." I was done with Lil Bit for the day.

When is your birthday?" [@ 3:35:45 pm 3-9-10] I asked Brit-Brit. There was no more gold mail received this day. By the end of the day I returned home from work. At the end of the night I start this game over. Better yet I progressively follow up with my key player; Janez. "What's up bay? I didn't know it was this late" [@1:09:56 am 3-10-10]. I fibbed. It is the beginning of the day and the game must continue. "Dra! What's up bro" [10:15:26 am]? This is my sister, Tiffany. She is only speaking. Plus she is graduating from UTK (University of Tennessee Knoxville) in a couple of months. Maybe I was still asleep when this gold mail arrived. I probably read, smiled, and went back to sleep.

VIII

I don't have to get up as early as first shift. So, like any regular weekend I would sleep until it hurts to close my eyes. When this happens you really don't have a choice except rise and shine. Usually it's about ten, eleven, on a good day, twelve. With a schedule like mine you could get up as early as seven o'clock. You could smoke a blunt. You could drink a beer. Try both (lol). It's just like listening to your hype song before running onto the football field. It's considered game time when twelve o'clock hit or even the first sign of gold mail.

Something all athletes should know; never engage in any strenuous physical activity without proper food source. Never eat right before you step on the field. Never eat heavy before you take a swim. Last but not least, never text on an empty stomach. Try this and you will see why.

Well I've had my wake and bake, but today is just a regular day. "I guess I go through this dumb-shit with you again (emoticon licking out tongue). Dig that" [12:32:24 pm]! I told Brit-Brit. It's common to send a text and get no reply. To avoid the silent treatment or the frustration I would simply follow up from the day before. Considering that we work together; hell, why not talk about work? "Did you ever get your Pizza Inn T-shirt? I got mine." I said. "Yes." She replied. "I'm reading." She said. Whatever she was reading I know it didn't have anything to do with me, but I like to joke a little. "Read this dis-ick in your bis-ack on page sexy eight and sixty nine, lol!" Everybody can't crack a sex joke. She obviously felt this was funny. "Lol." She replied. It seems she didn't get the joke. "Huh?" She said. "You like how this sound?" I asked. I continued with the excitement. "What are you reading? I asked a rhetorical question

22

and replied, "Karma Sutra?" This is the reason she never text me again. I apologized later. I guess I'm back in someone else's corner again.

Only this time I'm soliciting words without the harassment. "Smoke something-pimp" [@ 1:41:53pm]! I told Allison. There was no reply. I even tried calling and there was no answer. Before my afternoon ended I escaped my misery by apologizing to Brit-Brit. "I'm just kidding. When are you coming to the country" [1:50:29 pm]? I added. It was just yesterday...

IX

It was just yesterday when Lil Bit gave me the cold shoulder. I gave her the old ultimatum later the next night. "This is the last chance to keep a friend. I said. "Lets' go to the movies and leave a space between us so I don't smell your hot breath. We should watch Our Family Wedding Celebration" [8:47:53 pm]! If this isn't a way to start shit, then I don't know who is winning. "No. And what did I tell you" [*Sexy-Red*]? She replied. Of course this was a new day. Maybe she had developed a little more tolerance. Maybe she liked this game? I don't know. I do know one thing. I waited for about two hours before I said anything else about the damn movies. "The movie hasn't even come out yet." I said with a nonchalant attitude. "Please don't be cruel and inconsiderate? I'm being nice. How about some courtesy" [10:53:21: pm]? I begged. Not a minute later, she said, "No" [*Sexy-Red*].

I just left it alone. About thirty minutes to my surprise, she followed up with a reason not to go to the movies. "I don't want to go to the movies with you. You is too short, now [*Sexy-Red*]" [11:26:34 pm]. I looked at the phone and I laughed. I didn't respond right away. I was probably watching television the whole time. I know I was doing something conducive to learning. This is something my high school Spanish teacher (Senora Flippin) would tell the class to keep us from goofing off. It was about 11:40: pm toward the end of the night when I sent another nonchalant message. It read, "could you be Lil Bit and not insensitive" [11:44:37 pm]?

I was under the impression that her negative comments bothered me. I want her to know that her sarcasm was not all ironic, but original. She still didn't get the last word. I'm awake during the sleepiest hours of the night and texting is only fun when you are not very busy. What better time to expect a little fantasy? I say before bed. I turned my charm up a notch right before bed. Urgent messaging is equivalent to fishing with a drowned worm only to be nibbled on by top water minnows feeding at the bottom of the lake in shallow water.

They say food is the key to a man's heart. This is true in so many ways. If food is the key to my heart, then a woman's brain is a master key. I have no key. I'm only equipped with brains and deception. "It is late and I am hungry. What did you eat today"[@2:40:20 am 3-11-10]? I said.

I went to sleep after that. I laid in bed programming ringtones for the incoming messages and phone calls. I downloaded ringtones and cleared memory space until I fell asleep. Thanks for technology, but picking a combination lock wasn't my gift. This night I went to sleep without any gold mail.

I didn't use my phone the next morning. It was late in the afternoon or close to the evening when I did. Who knows? I probably tried to get some… Well that is personal. It was past three- thirty when I decided to follow up with the latest message. No one sent any gold mail. It's left up to me to kick this game off again. It's like the game of Four-Square. I played Four-Square in elementary. The objective: Do not let the ball bounce in your territory twice after the first bounce. It consists of four people each standing in one big square. The square divides into four smaller squares. Each person has to protect his or her own square. Then a kick-ball bounces into the entire square landing in anyone's territory. An under hand volley ball motion is gently used to tap the ball to an opponent's square. If the objective fails, then you are out of the game.

I guess I fall into Lil Bit's corner first. "See, this is a good time you should be up." I told her. "You got enough time to cook or get something to eat. You got enough time to run or go to the gym and still be on time for work" [3:36:27 pm]. I continued. "Lol. "Whatever" [*Sexy-Red*].

I went to work later this evening and found that we had a new manager. We had about five or six different managers during my stay at Pizza Inn. Mrs. Terry was the third manager to run the store. She kind of had a high school teacher's personality. Mrs. Terry could tolerate anything as long as her little office didn't keep her hid from making pizzas and greeting customers. I liked her best of all the managers. All she wanted was dependable workers. All who worked her shift were dependable. Most had rather conflicting schedules or just couldn't make it to work. I volunteered to be Mr. Dependable. I told Manager Terry if anyone has to take a day off or can't make it to work, then I'll work. I didn't have as much going on as everybody else except for the desperate need for money. Hell, I got past bills due. I worked the least amount of days, but most hours in a single day about three days a week.

The next night I text Lil Bit after work. I stayed on the subject about food for some reason. "I forgot to tell you what I ate" [12:19:48 am]. I explained. I stayed up late this night or must have tossed and turned due to the dead silence of the phone. I lay in bed watching DVD's probably buzzed up on some beer. The movie credits had rolled and returned to the main menu. As I forced myself to get up and shut off the power, I checked my phone and noticed the last message I intended to send was still on the screen. This time it was 3:18:48 am when I sent, "never mind." I hope that Lil Bit understands I am not even mad and food really isn't the subject anymore. "Never- mind what" [*Sexy-Red*] [3:19:28am]? She spontaneously asked. "Just thinking… [3:25:01 am]" I replied. We are finally talking again. Let's just say now I got your attention, might as well get something good out of the situation.

I tried to think of something funny, something that would make her laugh. I tried to think of something mean that wouldn't make her mad. I figured cracking a joke would be my best route. "Joke: You are so skinny, you can stand in the rain and not get wet; but you are so tall you can poke the cloud and make it rain" [3:38:08 am]! She wasn't mad, but about two minutes later she sure didn't send me a Lol. "That wasn't even funny you little short shit" [*Sexy-Red*]! I bet she went to sleep with a smile on her face. I read the message and left it on the screen until day break.

X

I woke up, at 10:33:39 am with some gold mail sent from my manager, telling me to call her. "Call me. This is Mrs. Terry" [sent from my HTC TILT? 2a Windows? Phone from AT&T]. She had a great big signature. I called her right away. She needed to know if I could come in and make some pizza dough. I made it in about 11:30 am. I went straight to whipping the dough. Business was a little slow during the one o'clock and two o'clock hours. Instead of me asking to leave early, I just sat around waiting for the phone to ring. All of the orders were single personal pan pizza orders. I really didn't have to budge, but I did get back on the subject of food with Lil Bit. I don't think I ever teased her this bad. It was breakfast my step mother had prepared and I wanted to give Lil Bit the most vivid picture to make every description an imagination as if it were prepared before her, "Pancakes smothered in honey, fried biscuits, salmon & rice topped with sautéed onions, bacon & scrambled eggs with a splash of orange juice on the side! "Damn this was yesterday's breakfast. "The only thing missing was you, my sweet red hot toothpick" [1:29:54 pm]! I was done about 1:00 pm, but I stayed and took ticket orders till about 4pm.

I don't understand taking so long to respond to a message, but I can only think of two reasons. One is busy. The other is anonymous for several reasons. She replied with the same shit about an hour later, requesting her demands from two days ago. Only this time she had a different signature which indicated independence. "Stop texting my phone. Why you so fucking hard headed? [*I CAN ONLY DO ME*]? I didn't send a text to anybody for the rest of the day.

In fact, the next day I was up as early as ten o'clock. I ask my mom indirectly if I could impregnate one of these females. "Hello darling, the sweetest woman in the word. "Let' say spring wins again! It's pretty outside. Why aren't you planting, what's pretty and blooms? Is this the season to plant the, seed?" [@9:54:35am3-13-10]. My mom knows I have a gift-for-gab, so I was really speaking. She actually answered. "Hello son." Mom said. "Lol. "Yep, you in a good mood and nope it's rainy, in the 40's here; had pretty spring days last week. Ok, come and help me plant. How are you? Love ya. "Miss ya." Mom said.

I went back to sleep with a clear head. I awake with clear thoughts only to think of Janez. "What's up lil buddy? "Good morning!" It was past morning, well past noon. I didn't know how to greet Lil Bit as a normal person, so I tried to greet her as if she was Janez. "Good morning! "How are you today?" I asked Lil Bit. I didn't get a reply soon enough, so I called Crystal G's phone; and I knew that was a blank call.

Around about two o'clock, some shocking gold mail popped up with Crystal G's number, but it didn't look like her words. As a matter of fact I think some guy was screening her calls. "Don't know who you are, but you got the wrong number partner." Crystal G said. Janez responded to my greeting and told me, "hi." She always came through at the right time. When it seems that everyone bounces me from corner to corner she saves the game by being the last one standing with the ball awaiting new challengers.

"You know exactly who I am. "I'm just not sure if I know you partner." Argument escalates. "Na playa, "Don't text this phone again." I not only received gold mail. With the uncertainty of who was sending messages from Crystals phone I had to protect my charm. She wasn't the receiver, evidently. "Are you a girl or a female? I asked. "If you are a dude, then speak up and stop wasting your time!" I added. Lil Bit sent me some gold mail while waiting on a reply. She critiqued my greeting and compared to previous texts. "Yeah, your text is a lot better" [*I CAN ONLY DO ME*].

Crystal G's hot- gold mail popped up again. "I'm a nigga fool and I told your ass to stop hitting my damn phone up!" By this time the whole conversation has turned into a flaming pot of alphabet soup, a real argument that had me laughing, but saw no signs of winning. My last message of the day had to be a screen cracking window breaking jaw jacking heart breaker. "Don't expect me to bitch up!" All I'm saying is somebody should have let their voice be heard. This is how you get pissed off.

I went to work that evening and I worked with my shift leader Brit-Brit. She was craving ice cream the whole night for some reason. I ignored that subject and continued working. I finally ended my shift about eleven o'clock. I waited for five minutes and my dad pulled up. I was in a rush to get home, but I wasn't driving. When we got home, my dad gave me a beer and he went in the house. He left me the keys to the truck so I could listen to the radio. I rolled me a blunt, drank my beer, smoked my blunt and listened to 102.5 FM, Keith Sweat Radio. I was feeling pretty damn good. It's about one in the morning. I thought of who I could call, but the songs the radio played made me feel bad. For a moment I just became overwhelmed with apologies. I only made one apology, but it wasn't to whom you think deserved it. "My; bad. "I got excited with those phone calls and text you made. I Apologized to Lil Bit. "Holler at you later. "Is this cool" [1:34:22 am 3-14-10]? I added.

I prepared myself for a non – reply reception. It didn't matter if she did or not. I aired out. I went in the house. I put my phone on the charger. I played a DVD consisting of 4 or 5 different movies. I went to sleep. I slept until 1:00 pm. I rolled another blunt. I got my day started. I did not well I do not focus on texting when I'm out doing my thing. I do something conducive to learning. I didn't have to work today. I made this day off a tribute to yesterday's temptation… I remember the words Ice cream. I diffused the consequence of temptation. It's like I weighed ice cream in a cone in one hand and the temptation in my mouth all because of my mannish thoughts. "Did you get your ice cream yet? You got me wanting some too" (emoticon tongue out eyes facing text) [@ 7:20:26 pm]! Laughing at Brit-Brit; no more messages; think…

After the fighting words boiled down, I started to make them simmer up again. "I'm a n-i-g-g-a fool. I told your ass to stop hitting my damn phone up!" I forwarded the hot gold mail. "Oh yeah; you would say something like that with your country ass." I continued. This message is sent to Crystal G on March 15, 2010 @ 1:06 am. I called Lil Bit… There was no answer.

I got plenty rest after I made that call. I probably went to the moon. My first text was a reminder to Lil Bit. "Hi. "I called you late last night." I did not get a reply. I sent a text to Crystal G again at about five o'clock. I wanted to fuck-with-whoever-the-hell screened her calls. "What up dude? "Where is that good weed?" Evidently this next message clearly tells me that somebody is actually fucking-with-me. The gold mail popped up. "Nigga, I'm telling you one more time to stop texting you faggot as bitch [5:10:56 pm kml Lolol… They suddenly scorched the pot of gold mail, turning it into hot lava. If you pull a cat by the tail, then you get scratched. When you scorch a pot of beans, you can't tastefully eat them. When you engulf hot food it burns the tongue. Try to feed a vicious dog. Stick your hand in his bowl and see what happens. I felt like Max, the dog in the movie; Mans best Friend. Instead of morphing into chameleons, lions, and bears; it was like a computer flashing… Warning! Maximum overload! Self-destructing in 10…9…8…7…6…5…4…3…2…1… It was more like a ten minute time bomb with ten seconds remaining. I waited exactly ten minutes to reply…

"Who; and what the fuck is you? You-blood-sucking-Maggot! Get off that dust and calm your words! I'm sucker free! Stop hating! You dirty mouth souse! Lol if you want to [5:20:49 pm]! I exploded and just went the fuck-off. I destroyed the screened caller because they never called nor text again. I obliterated the text threat and prepared to go to work. "Call Pops; ready for work" [5:37:28 pm] I sent text to Maurice.

XI

I try not to forget about the people who fell off in the game. It's just like the friends who grew close and distant. You should have a clue by now. You should know who stays, who goes, and who is gone. These people are gone with the sender, gone with the receiver, gone with the wind, gone with the wicked ways of the world; gone with a new slate; gone with a get a life attitude; gone with a thought thinking outside the box; gone with the idea, I'm not coming back; gone with a trail of erasers erasing their tracks as if they were drawing with every step made; gone with a point of no return.

XII

After leaving work that night I didn't care who got mail. I didn't care who sent mail. The next morning Janez spoke and I was probably at work early at nine that morning making pizza. "Hey friend" [11:40:45 am 3-16-10]. She was on Spring Break.

I didn't respond until the next day. "What's going on my friend? "How is your spring break" [10:36:48 pm 3-17-10]? I added. I sent Lil Bit the same text. The only difference is I asked her in reference to her grammar schooled kids. "What's going on my friend? How is Spring Break" [10: 38: 12pm]? "Good." She said. Janez replied immediately after Lil Bit and answered, "it's, good!" "How are you doing today?" I asked Lil Bit. "What you got up for the weekend?" I continued. "I'm free until five o'clock tomorrow." I informed her [2:02:42 pm 3-19-10]. "I don't know yet *I can only do me*." She replied. Later that evening, past the 8 o'clock hour, Maurice hit my phone indicating he had a hot date. "I'm about to go to the movies" [8:40:35 pm]. Maurice stated. He must have had a secret admirer. I'm assuming he did. "You, and who?" I asked. "No body, but somebody might meet me there" 8:56:59 pm]. Lil bro had a secret admirer that night.

It's been 1hr.30min; almost two hours past and I'm at home trying to get me a date. Lol. I called Allison. She didn't answer. I called twice and she still didn't answer. It's like I'm right back where I started, bouncing around like some kick ball. These are players in the game who won't win. In other words they keep playing the game, neglecting other contenders. "When do you answer your phone?" I asked Allison. "I don't." Rapidly, responding. These days a text message is more concrete than a phone call because I called her twice and didn't get a single answer, but I text her once and got a simple reply immediately. "Well, how you gonna know where the green at" [10:06:07 pm]? I asked furiously. Little did she know; I had the herb. I was the weed man. I was on my grind. I wasn't the big man, but I was hustling, struggling, striving, spending, saving, and surviving. She didn't respond. I became angry. "You must got company?" I said. There was no reply. To hell with this chick, I thought.

I'm steady bouncing around. I'm back in Brit-Brit's corner. She's a contender. I sent her some cool points. "Cool points" [10:28: pm]! Twenty minutes later she responded wandering what the cool points were for. "For what" 10:47:48 pm? She wondered.

I sent Lil Bit a text at midnight. "You gonna call me tonight" [12:36:13 am 3-20-10]? My phone rang about 8 minutes till 1am. "You think you're cooler than me" by Mike Posner, was the ringtone. I knew it wasn't Lil Bit because my phone is programmed to play specific ringtones for certain people. "You think you're cooler than me" is programmed as a business tone alert. "Can you pull an open-to-close- tomorrow" [12:52:00 am]? Mrs. Terry asked. I responded as soon as I checked this message. "Yes. It's possible" [12:52:00 am]. I answered. "Be there at 9am; thank you" [12:57:02]. I guess I remain Mr. Dependable in her agenda mate. Lil Bit finally responded with confirmation about an hour later. "I will call you tomorrow. I got a tooth ache and I got off early tonight" *I can only do me*.

I went to work that morning and clocked in at 9:00am. I was supposed to work a double-shift. Considering business was slow, I was asked to leave at 5:00pm by Shift Manager. I called Mrs. Terry to tell her I left early. "I tried to call. I was supposed to work 9am to 11pm. I worked from 9am until 5pm" [6:26:27pm]. "Thanks. "Who came in for you?" Mrs. Terry asked. I really wanted to complain because I worked with the meanest shift manager in Collins Mississippi. Miss J.W. Miss J.W was hired a few weeks after me. She was hired as a waitress. Miss J.W carried herself like a school teacher as well; the glasses; the proper English; and the kindness, to people who are her favorite. She was bumped up to a Shift Leader and treated me like a special case. Later she became manager and treated me like a trainee. Later I became unemployed. Lol.

I received unemployment benefits the time I realized my hours didn't even add up to part time. Working while receiving unemployment benefits is annoying, especially when you know you're not a fraud. Unemployment compensated me $50 a week, credited on a (EPIC) visa card. I became employed with Sanderson's Farm on March 15, 2011. This terminated my unemployment benefits. I was released from Pizza Inn by Manager Miss J.W. I went from flipping pizzas; to flipping chickens. This was a whole lot better income, but a lot of hard work… I had to digress a little, now back to the game.

XIII

I never told Mrs. Terry who actually came in to work for me. Hypothetically, no one came in to work for me. Do you get the big picture? However, this day actually starts later in the evening. I follow up with Lil Bit and her toothache condition. "Are you feeling any better" [6:26:27 pm]? I asked. I do the same thing every day. I do regular stuff like text or call some body simply to kill time. I sent Brit-Brit to follow up the cool points. "See; you are all by yourself and I don't have a good movie to watch like the one you're watching now" [6:49:40 pm].

I will never know what she does to play this game. It only took Lil Bit one hour, one minute to answer my question of concern. "Yeah I'm feeling better" *I can only do me*. She said. "Are you doing anything special today?" I asked immediately. It took only thirty five minutes for this reply. I sent Allison a text while I waited, "what's up" [8:05:10 pm]? She replied about one minute later. Her reply was a good reason, yet a happy excuse not to talk. She says, "Nothing; I'm in New Orleans" [8:06:06 pm]. Lil Bit announced, "going to the club *I can only do me*" 8:15:01 pm]. I called her phone the same minute. She did not answer, so I began the texting game. Really, thinking to myself; really? "Answer your phone" [8:16:37 pm]. I howled. She says, "I was on Face Book" *I can only do me* [8:18:50]. I say, "You see me" [8:27:29 pm]? No reply. She was trying to tell me why she didn't answer. I thought she found something about me on Face book. "You too gutta" [8:40:59 pm! I boasted. Two minutes later she states another condition. This will tend to happen to anyone, but you know… "Lol don't feel like talking. Sorry I got a headache" *I can only do me*. I got mad. The famous words of my late great trigonometry teacher (Mr. Bennet, better known as 'Ben-Ben) "Lies and Garbage" were very useful at this point. "Mane… Whatever!!! You are going to the club. I don't want to hear that shit" [8:45:17 pm]! It took me about thirty five minutes to calm down and I finally told her what I wanted. I say, "I wasn't trying to talk. I wanted you to come to FRIENDSHIP where I can see you before you go to the club" [9:23:40 pm]. This ended the conversation. Hell, she won.

XIV

It's getting late in this game something like baseball; World Series, Major League at the bottom of the 9th inning. The game is tied 0-0. Everybody is playing a good game making base hits, but defense prevails. Fresh new players enter the game from the back up roster. In this case, I'm the umpire. I call the shots.

About seven different players enter the texting game. Two are homeboys (cousins). One is a co-worker. One is a friendly customer who I met at work. One is a local who I met at the gas station. One is an older cousin who drove to Tennessee with Maurice. The other one is a home girl from Friendship.

Covoseia, the co-worker had recently started working night shift. He was a big time scorer for the Collins High School Basketball Team. A job and a basketball schedule with no one to work in your spot is kind of a conflict. It is easy to compare game days to scheduled work days, so that really wasn't the problem.

The conflict to be resolved is to get someone to work in his spot tonight. An urgent trip to Jackson is the reason. I don't believe anyone could really work in his place tonight. I get this message in the middle of the afternoon on my day off. "You feel like working tonight? "This is Covoseia" [2:06:44pm 3-21-10]. It took me about five minutes to answer. "Yeah. Call Mrs. Terry. Let her know; and holler back." I decided at 2:10:59 pm. "I'm in church right now. When I leave here I got to go back to Jackson and see if my grandmother is still in the hospital or not" [2:12:49]. He continued. I became very concerned. I knew for sure he wasn't working tonight. "You are closing, right" [2:19:22 pm]? I assumed.

There was no reply and I didn't hesitate to carry on with the business. "Am I having to close" [2:23:18pm]? I agreed to work in Corvoseia's shift. "I accept." I said [2:34:18pm]. I went to work and dealt with the consequences. However, Mrs. Terry was notified via telephone voice message.

I went back to work the next morning because I was actually scheduled to work this day. I worked from 9am-4pm. I got a message from Maurice that evening. "Cuz said call him at his new number 601-550-5039" [7:49:54 pm 3-22-10]. Maurice said. I called Rod about 8:00 pm. He didn't answer, but he sent a text. One pet peeve is to call someone and you text, who is this? "What's up? "Who is this?" Rod said with a signature, [.@.@?.&.@.@? give me that pussy](8:02:04pm). His signature is so blunt I can't give a straight answer. "This is Dick" [8:04:58 pm]. I said. "Who is this?"

He asked again. ([.@.@?.&.@.@? give me that pussy]) [8:06:07pm]? I answered right away. I told him who I was because I almost got carried away with the games. "Dra Fool" [8:06:46 pm]! Cuz knew it was me then. "What's up" [8:07:50 pm]? I called his phone again. He answered this time and we got it cracking talking about smoking weed.

Two days had passed. I worked the 23rd24th and the 25th. Some days my brother and I would work together. We would work under the Supervision of my step mother, his biological mother, Mother Josie. It's pretty interesting working with family. Most people say working with family will never work, but the New Millennium generated a lot of family owned businesses which is hard to become employed with. We worked the 25th at 9am until 4pm. Maurice prepared all the dough and I made pizzas. He made pizzas as well. Maurice received a phone call from some classmates from Class of 2008 during the day. They were close friends of his and wanted to get together and play a flag football game. I left work right after buffet hours which are from 11am until 2pm. "Want to play football today?" Maurice said [3:20:00 pm 3-25-10]. I'm used to playing Madden but, damn! I'm thinking I ain't cut out for this shit nomo.

I was at home feeling like, man are you serious? I didn't text back, but I called... We hit the Collins Baseball Field about 6pm. I had on my brown Dickie pants that I worked in. It was kind of cool and rainy that night so I had on an old brown-black and grey striped "Brick City" Turtleneck sweater from 2001. I didn't have any cleats. I had on all white Ree's (Reebok Classics). Maurice had on blue and white Under Armor apparel; black and white cleats and receiver catching gloves. There were enough bodies out there to hold two teams and maybe two players to substitute someone who got tired or got hurt.

Flag Football turned into two-hand-touch. Two-hand-touch turned into tackle. This is what I call football. I created a fumble, stripping the ball from an elusive running back who opposed me as one man to beat. I returned the fumble about ten yards before I was tackled ten yards outside the end-zone. Maurice scored a hand-off for the remaining ten yards. Later the quarterback connected with a receiver for a 25 yard post touchdown. As a team, we lost the game 35-14. We had lots of fun, but the pain made us pay for it the next day. Everybody went their own separate way after the game ended. Maurice and I went to the Jr. Food Mart. We bought PowerAde drank Gatorade and reminisced.

The next day… I woke up almost five minutes before 8:30 am; four minutes to be exact. Janez had school today and I would always think of something good to say to help us remember why we do this. The season was in the month of; what would be, warm, but cool. It was mostly chilly mornings and sunny afternoons; warm days and cool nights. Approximately, ten years earlier I was a junior in high school too. "I remember these days getting up early putting on fresh colognes, (Sean Jean, Unforgivable, Curve, Joop, Candie, Versace) smelling good, dressed down in uniform (Khakis & polo or Button-down with a tie). I imagine you look like cotton candy with the essence of peaches and cream!! Wake me up. I must be dreaming" [8:26:30 am]! Janez says, "No. You are not dreaming" [8:28:08 am].

Whatever I did today, I'm sure I started the day off right. I didn't work. In fact, I just collected a little gold mail. I got word that Pizza Inn has a mandatory meeting tomorrow, "FWD; Store meeting Saturday @ 3:00 pm. Must attend or fired" (11:20: 02 am)!!! This was forwarded by Maurice. I received this message twice. Mrs. Terry sent the same message seconds later. This was the original message before it was forwarded to me, "Store meeting Saturday @ 3:00 pm. Must attend or fired" [11: 20: 58 am]!!! I probably went to the meeting high. I didn't get high-and-then go to the meeting; I was already high from that morning; A typical day off. Everything was cool. Co-workers noticed, but I was attentive (asking questions and showing interest) and didn't notice them. I sent text my oldest brother (Lil Boo) later, to send me my cousin's phone number. "Send me BL's number" [6:11:09 pm]. I said. Instead of him sending me BL's number, my mom sent my other cousin, Cedrick's number. "This is Cedrick 423-498-6251" [7:16:18 pm]. Mom said.

XV

Mrs. Terry sent a reminder beginning the afternoon about today's meeting. She says, "Please don't forget about the meeting" [12:33:02 pm 3-27-10]. The meeting was focused on proper ways to set up the Salad Bar, proper cleaning of pizza pan lids, preparing pizza, pasta, and breadsticks for buffet hours, weighing all the toppings before placing them on pizza dough, cleaning/breaking down the Make Table, (station where pizzas are made) amount of water used to mix dough and pizza sauce; and last but not least cleaning and closing the store at normal closing hours. When the meeting opened for questions, I was concerned about the rush to leave and clock out after store closing hours. Some shift leaders treated closing hours like clocking out at the end of your shift. I hated closing…

The meeting turned out successful. Nothing changed about closing hours, but I was still happy to be on the schedule whenever scheduled to work. Mrs. Terry called the evening of the 28th. She notified me to call work, "call Pizza Inn" [5:21:56 pm 3-28-10]. I called. I was told that I needed to report to work April 1st 2010. I had about three days off, so within those 36hrs, I did what any vacation or suspension would allow before your return date. I smoke. I drank. The rest is preparation for the big work day.

April 1, 2010 came a lot faster than I thought. I gathered myself and my dad picked me up around 5:45pm. At 5:48:22 pm I received a message, "you better get her soon." Mrs. Terry ordered. It takes only 10 minutes to get there from my Dad's house. I made it there about 5:55pm and hit the clock at 5:58 pm and got my day on.

XVI

It's been about two weeks since I last heard from Lil Bit. Like I always do, I break the ice. I do it again and again. It is [April 3, 2010 1:53:55 am]. It must have been a night I had to close at work and made it out of there probably fifteen minutes after 12:00 midnight. I probably made it home about 12:30am, counting the time it takes to call my ride and clock out. Also, I had to drink my beer, smoke my blunt, and listen to the radio. Personally, it takes a person about an hour to unwind leaving work before going in the house. It's just not the same coming home from work entering someone else's domain. Starting your day is, sometimes challenging. Ending your day is, mostly sneaky. "I still miss you but, I am not mad at you." I told Lil Bit. There was no reply [1:53 am 4-03-10].

A week had passed. All I did is talk on the phone and made blank phone calls. I sent Lil Bit a text again on April 9, 2010 at 11:27: 06 am. I say, "so, how have life been treating you?" There was no reply. I called Janez later that afternoon. She sent a text back, "I'm at school bay" [1:38:39pm]. The day had passed with only this one piece of gold mail sent by Janez. We talked on the telephone around 10:00 pm for about an hour. She had to get ready for the next day...

It is midnight and I remember Lil Bit's birthday is on the tenth. I sent her a message using nothing but numbers; number's (1-177155-400). This is a number code revealing "I miss you". It was used back-in-the-day on pagers and beepers. "You should be sending me a message like 1-177155-400." I told her. There was still, no gold mail. I waited until the afternoon to see if I would get any gold mail morning messages... I did not. Finally, I sent text, "Happy Birthday, from Text Buddie." I told

Lil Bit. "I'm seeing you tonight right" I asked 12:19:20 pm? She finally replied saying, "Thanks." She says, "I'm still laying down (with another signature that read [*100% GORGEOUS*] 12:43pm]. I used to joke with her. It seems that laughter and humorous messages would be the only way she would communicate. "Get your gorgeous ass up and call my phone." I said [@1:30:03 pm]. I don't know what made everything sound so real, but she would joke right back. At 2:01 pm she says, "I need an outfit. "Are you offering to buy me one (100% GORGEOUS)?" I don't believe real relationships last long with jokes because eventually somebody is going to pull somebody's card, expecting something for real. It's like throwing a curve ball to a no-pitch-hitter. You look the ball all the way in until it curve towards you creating an altered since of judgment. You step out of the batter box and watch the ball hit the catcher's mit; Pop! ST—RIKE! You don't want to get hit by the ball and you don't want to swing at a ball that appears to be outside of the strike zone. Just contemplate quick decisions. I say, "I'll get you an outfit but, it won't be today. Just let me stay all night for a birthday present, lol."

The next few gold mail pop-ups were all mine. I valued these like the Leprechaun cherished his gold. I guess I got my talk game up on the phone. I had met this real dark chocolate girl at work. She had a smile that just growled at me. She was a customer coming in to buy pizza. She gave me her number and I was there to take Shanika's order. I got her number the night of Lil Bit's birthday. I called Shanika the next day. Gold mail Pop up! She sent a text back. She says, "What's up" [4:06:21 pm 4-11-10]? She called me immediately after she sent her text. We talked and carry on for the week. A good week without texting; as contradicting as it sounds is a good week of live conversation. Janez would always get her time in no matter what. You have to keep in mind when time changes, age will progress.

I get a piece of gold mail on April 17, 2010 at 9:45 in the morning. It seems like it's been a while since I got mail this early. "You know to come to work this morning right?" Mrs. Terry requested. Apparently, I didn't know. I didn't reply either. I went to work at 11 o'clock like a regular work day; no questions, no comments. Clock in and carry on.

About three or four days had passed and I call Shanika. For some odd reason she would always answer my phone call with a text message.

I didn't like it but, it was considered gold mail. I remain the player who initiates the phone call. If she answered, then we had a cordial conversation. "Hey, can you just text me?" Shanika asked [10:56:37: pm 4-21-10]. I got my gold mail. I did not text back. I called Allison next. She sent text back the next morning, "You called last night." I did not text until I accepted why I haven't heard from Janez. "What's up? It's been a long time since I heard from you. Are you doing okay?" I asked [12:13:40 pm 4-26-10]. No reply. I sent text to Shanika, "What's up?" [12:28:37 pm]. I sent text to Lil Lil Bit at 5:42:50 pm. "I'm texting your ass all day. So, what up lil buddy? I'm missing your fine-red-apple-head-ass." I teased. "Shit." I grumbled... No reply. I sent text to Shanika again, "What up" [5:48 pm"]? No reply. Either people are real busy or they just don't feel this game no more. I actually didn't receive any gold mail for a week straight. I sent all the text until April 30; literally May 4, metaphorically begging for gold mail. There were a lot of small conversations between these messages. I'm just being honest.

A few days had passed. I worked some and I chilled-out more. I talked to Lil Bit late the night of the 28th. We talked for a while and the phone had just hung up. By late midnight around 1:43:36 am, I sent a text to Lil Bit, "I was still on the phone when you hung up." I said. Day break broke in that morning. I woke up and watched a movie and stayed in bed. "Come lay in bed with me." I told Lil Bit [9:53 am]. She never text me back.

I went to work at four o'clock the next day. I got off early at 7:00 pm. "A, I'm through. I done clocked out." I told Maurice. "Mane, come get me if you haven't left yet. I got off at 7." I said [8:13:42 pm 4-30-10]. I stayed around for like an hour and thirty minutes because I was expecting to be off at ten. I had to wait on a ride so I just hung around and sent mail. I sent text to the same people. Shanika and Lil Bit received the same message like a minute behind each other; which said, "Shanika, am I talking to you tonight" [9:47:58 pm]? No reply. "Lil Bit, am I talking to you tonight" [9:48:28 pm]? No reply. I tell Janez, "Damn baby I know you have been busy but, I have been trying to call you. What's going on?" I asked [9:54:41 pm]. No reply.

XVII

I went to Ramey's Grocery Store May 1, 2010. It's located in Covington County Collins. Of all the people I could have seen, I saw Brit-Brit. She was in the store with her Mom and Dad. I expected to get a hug or some kind of friendly handshake. She didn't initiate the gesture so, I spoke smiled and gave her the sideways look like; I can't get a hug? I was kind of happy seeing her in public other than seeing her at work. I confronted her later that evening, "Oh; I couldn't get a hug in front of Pops" [9:47:07 pm]. No reply.

I was ready to smoke the next hour. I sent text to my boy Don G, "Call my phone-need some green?" Meanwhile waiting on Don G to call, I checked back In with Lil Bit. "Who is my girl mad at today?" I asked. "I wish you were mad at me so I could make it up to you. I continued. Don G drove over my Dads house in his blue four-door Chevy Cavalier and called me from outside. I came outside and we rolled out. We went to visit the moon and the stars lol. While on the moon I called a surprised co-worker whom I had become subordinate to when she received a promotion. That's-right- Miss J.W. I was so far in space I felt I could reach out to anybody. I called her. We talked but, it was a short conversation which ended with her telling me, "Don't call my phone any more, boy." It was shocking, of course but, it was funnier than anything. We made it back to earth about 2:00 in the morning. Hypothetically speaking, I arrived at home at 2:00 am. I had an appetite that would cook meals with every breath I took. What a surprise to see pizza sitting on the table? I ate about 3 or 4 slices of pizza, some cheese sticks, chicken-wings and washed it down with some kool-aid. No need for beer. I cut off the kitchen lights and silently walked to my room. I ate chips for a snack while watching a movie. About 3Am I was ready to sleep like a baby but, first thing's first; this game doesn't stop at the sight of the moon. May 2, 2010 3:38:40 am I checked J.W for trying to kick me off the moon (blow my high). "Oh, I understand. We're just business partners, right?" I didn't expect a reply. I just wanted her to know and now I feel better.

I didn't work the actual day on May 2, but Maurice did. He would get off late and I would try to time him the days I didn't work. "A bro, bring a mini-cigarillo" [11:56:08 pm]. And-damn, my timing was off. He had already made it home. I guess I won't see any moon and stars tonight. Lol lol, but it's not funny.

I still chilled. I did what I normally do as far as being at the crib. I sat outside in my Dad's truck listening to the radio drinking the beer he had left for me. Listening to 102.5 JKX Keith Sweat Radio always reminds you of a girl you once knew. The songs he would play brought back memories of a setting that takes place in your teenaged years. One particular R&B artist who has been around for a long time with tracks like "Bump and Grind", you remind me of "My Jeep", and 12-Play, which could never air on regular radio because of the lyrical content (explicit lyrics). "I'm listening to it "seems like you're ready" by R. Kelly." I told Lil Bit [1:08 am 5-03-10]. No reply. I personally reminisced to too many memories while listening to the radio. I thought forget it and went in the house. Sleep was good and gold mail was empty.

Later that evening I chilled with my homies (cousins) Don, Lil Don, Keyes Maurice (brother) and family. We drank beer and barbeque and hangout until someone pass out drunk. It's usually me or Don G. Lil Don (Don G little brother) flips out on the whole crew and take the whole scene.

I had a home-girl who stayed up the street from my Dads house. She would always turn a boring day or a wasted night into a dramatic moment. She would yell to the top of her lungs so that you know you can hear. She uses that tone of voice on her Nephews (Keon and Aaron) and her friends that pick on her; but she's cool. Meet Half-Pint. Half Pint is a nickname that says half pint. She's short, a little taller than me of course; thick hips and Chinese eyes. She just pops of like a cork of champagne.

I went home around 9:00 pm. "What up?" I sent text to Half Pint [9:07 pm]. No reply; probably just a phone call, a drunken conversation, and a drama free night.

My gold mail started to get shorter and shorter by the day. I sent a lot of messages and met a lot of players who didn't really dig this game. Most of the interaction with them was face to face, either in the neighborhood or on the phone. One thing for sure is everybody who smokes weed, smokes to pass time alleviating a boring or hectic situation. Staying in the country with a part time job, no vehicle and living with parents in your late twenties is not something I would call "Good Times". During these times you have to make fun with what you got, good times.

Cell phones, distant cousins, bootleggers and weed are all resources for habitat in the country. If you didn't have a cell phone, someone might pull up in your driveway and honk his horn. The closest store is about 3-5 miles west and the convenient store is about 7-10 miles east. Therefore, it is not just a hop and a skip to make a trip to the store.

"Survival" is the name of the game living in the country is what my Dad always said. A trip to the store would consist of rounding up two or more people. Collins was considered a dry county before 2012. They could not sell any beer or alcoholic beverages. Only gas, tobacco products, good food and snacks were sold. By 2012, they finally passed a law to veto the dry county rule. Now everyone who drinks beer can get it in Covington County instead of driving to other counties miles away from your home. These happy days are considered good times. You still had to drive 15-20 miles to the next county to get liquor. We make store-runs, beer trips, liquor stops, and smoke a lot of weed. This is how you have fun in the country. This is our survival.

XVII ¼

The game kind of takes a turn this quarter. It turns from gold mail to regular G-mail. It's about business and survival. I introduced you to the survival tactics that we use. Now I will illustrate how we do-it. Any given day is always a quest in the form of survival whether staying at home, camping in the woods, hiking up a mountain, hunting, fishing, or touring a different city. In other words, you have to have proper tools and equipment to prepare for such a journey.

We were not just coping in the sticks. "This is Dra. "Are you straight?" I asked Don G [4:47:20 pm 5-04]. When you ask a person, "Are you straight" It could mean three things. It means; "Do you need something?" It means; "Are you holding something?" Also it means; "Are you ok?" Ironically speaking, "Do you have some weed?" He sent no reply. About an hour, approximately 1 hr 15 min, I sent text again, "Are you at the crib?" He sent no reply. "Meet me at the crib." I said. I never heard from Don G the whole day. This is survival tactic number one. If you don't have any positive feed-back, then don't answer your phone.

My Mom sent a photo she had taken at work (Rossville Convalescent Center) on May 5, better known as "Cinco de Mayo (A traditional Holiday celebrated by the Spanish Tribe. She and her company dressed up and celebrate the tradition. "I see you rocking the sombrero or "Sunday hat". "Yo mi gusta Seniorita!" I said [4:40:16 pm]. "Today was a good day" (Ice Cube).

Midnight came as late as 12:55:23 am and I was toasted from earlier that day. It was a dead-end kind of night. No phone calls. No gold mail; just alcohol and weed. I still feel good enough to send a message so, I sent text to Lil Bit, "I forgot how to text. I am intoxicated." I said. I tried to use reverse psychology and it didn't even work. No reply.

XVII ½

Two whole days had slowly faded away. I had run out of my product which was a good thing. Unlike the police shutting down your everyday house party, we used the trailer as our own hangout spot. Madden Football and NBA 2K were the games that kept the spot jumping. Taadka Vodka is the cheap shit that gets you past drunk. Bud-Ice, Bud Light and Bud Weiser are the best choice for a thirst quencher. Occasionally I would hit the scene only wanting to smoke. The rest of the crew would be half faded from the beer and alcohol; and weed. I kept me a lil personal stash because I know me. We all know personal stashes don't last long and this is why we call out to re-up or stay lifted. Dad didn't like this activity in his yard. The drinking was ok. The weed was questionable. The crowd… Lets get back to the game.

"Come outside" [2:00:05 pm/ 5-07-10]. Don G pulled up at the right time. Parents were gone to work. It's early in the afternoon and no one to fail our deception of running shit our way. These days make being dependent very advantageous. Don G was about 18 -19 years old. I was about 25-26. We got fucked up every chance we could. He would supply most days when he call. I would supply on days when I call and catch a ride.

In the country you got to get yours or you're just assed-out. I would retrieve a personal bag and wouldn't call for a couple days or however long I could manage. "Nig I'm outside" [2:06:36 pm/ 5-10-10]. Today I was the supplier. Plus I owed a lil fee from the other day. Don G says, "I will be over Keyes crib. "I'm about to ride by Jones right now. Jones is a Community College in Laurel, MS, my birth place. Don G was taking classes doing his own thing. We got right that day and always remember never go home without it.

"You got me bro"[1:05:44pm/ 5-11-10]? I reply, "Smoke something." I just ignored the debt call, but it was more like an advantage on surviving the times. "Aint no smoke?" "Yeah I got some... Oh... Alright bro..." He said. He must have remembered how we roll. "Are you in Friendship?" I reported back. "Yep." He showed up and we turned up.

Sometimes I'm humbuggish just to see whats going on, not like the police. I must have called Don G phone only to find out I'm still at home and they ass at the club. "I'm in the club" [12:39:49am 5-12-10]. I called T. Grey phone too. He replies, "In party. "What up?" "Leave that bitch and smoke something." I was either bored or waking up. "Where you at?" T. Grey asked. "In the hood." "Which one?" We by the trap." "Yeah." Confused me. I didn't have a clue they were at the same spot and T. Grey didn't have a clue who he was talking to. I guess I felt stranded in the country. "You headed to the crib?" I asked Don G. T.Grey was so fucked up he just did recognize my number. It had been a while since I hit em up. "Who is this? "What? "You switched numbers or something?" I wasn't trying to hear that drunk shit. I say, "No. "Are you in Hattiesburg too!" "Yeah." "Is Lil Bro with you?" I asked. "Who?" T Grey said [2:27am]. Those cats hung tough.

I was in preparation to go to Tennessee. Tiffany would be graduating from UTK in a couple days. Mom made plans to pick me up in Laurel and Dad would drive me there to meet up with her. Mostly, I would chill in my room and setup this texting game. Mom text me and told me she was on her way to Mississippi, "leaving now." She said (12:13:27 pm). Traveling from Mississippi to Tennessee and vice versa had become a routine trip since a kid. Mississippi was home and Tennessee was home away from home. The normal 6hr trip had broken down to 4 to 5 hours depending on traffic and who was with you while driving. "I'll see you about 6 or 7pm?" I said. "Yes."

I remember talking to my cousin BL on the phone. I learned that he was a Mason Brother. He told me he had a business party and I suggested a DJ he had asked for. "You still need a DJ?" I was in the midst of packing my clothes still trying to get me something to keep me blowed when I arrive in Tennessee. "You got smoke?" I asked Don G. "How much?" He replied. I never really purchased less than a quarter of an ounce. I don't think I needed that much once I hit Tennessee, just enough to get me through the night and hopefully let my brothers EL and Lil Boo make me put it back in my pocket and smoke some Paya. "What you got up?" I sent text to T Grey.

I don't think BL recognized my number or programmed it in his phone because I text him. He finally replied answering, "Yeah. "Who is this?" T Grey replies, "Whatever. what up?" He knew what time it was plus he always had a lil extra like some Promethazine or a different type of kush. I sent the message for my cousin to DJ Fats. "This's Dra from the Ship. "My cousin BL will call you about some business (party)." I kept BL alert in case he would call. "This's Dra. "His name is DJ Fats. "His number is 601-826-0425." "Buss-up." I told Don G. BL accepted the message, "Ok." Don G finally scooped me up. Instead of T Grey coming to me, we went to him. "We're going to buss-up in a minute." "Who is this?" He said. "Dra." I replied. "What up-wit-it?" He asked. "Trying to smoke. I'm waiting on Don G so we can buss to the store." We probably had to get cigars etc. "I'm coming thru." He insists. Don G pulled up in the mean-time. "We fixin-to ride to the store. We gon be there.

I guess T. Grey changed his mind and decided to wait on us, wait on us at his crib. "Come thru, over here. Yeah." We clicked up and did our thing. I put packing on hold for a little while.

"I'll be in Meridian about 45 minutes." Mom said [4:02:33pm] "Ok. I'm packing." "Do I come through Laurel or..." We hadn't left from Collins because it's only a 30 minute ride. Mom must have put foot on the gas because she was in laurel before 6:00. "I'm here off Chantilly the store." She said [6:09:15pm].

One thing that could piss a person off the most is showing up late to a designated area. Mom didn't get mad this time but, I could tell she was frustrated like any normal moment of furry that over comes a situation. "We're leaving now" [6:10:21pm]. "What? You should have been left." I had to stall before replying because Daddy was flying down the highway and Mom was right. I should have been left. "Yes. "You're at the Texaco? "We're pulling up right now" [6:45:45]. "Yes. "Ok." We made the plan work. We met in Laurel at the store. About 7:00pm we were back on the road to head 59N a straight shot to Tennessee, through Alabama.

Two smooth hours of riding went easy exiting the state of Mississippi. "What you got going?" T. Grey said. "Riding through Bama." I replied. "Say that. "Get at me when you get back." "Bet." T. Grey checked on me the whole trip. "Where you at now cuz?" It's about 9:50 and we were half way there cruising through Alabama. "Birmingham." "Damn. "You'll never get home." He thought wise-cracking. "Where you at?" "On the moon." He said [10:02:49 pm]. "Hell yeah. "The Purple Drank was skrait." I continued. "Ha say that." "On that Kush, huh?" I inquired. "Reggie Miller." He said graphically.

XVII ¾

It's a different time-zone in Tennessee. We are like an hour faster than Mississippi, so the times between sending and receiving messages switched up on me. I didn't realize this little mishap until I started documenting the script.

"What up Half Pint? "I'm in Chatt" [11:27:53 pm]. No reply. "Are you still in Bama?" Asked T Grey. "Nope. "I'll be in Chatt about 50 mi" [11:46:20 pm]. "Yeah." "What kind of green on the moon?" I answer my own joke. "It aint. Its too damn high." He says, "none homie. It's empty up here, just craters-and-rocks-and-shit."

Me and Moms finally made it to the house round 1'something in the morning. I removed my duffle bag and got settled in. The next hour I was rollin-up. I went and sat outside on the back yard deck and started sending out crazy text messages. Of course I hit up T Grey and my brother first. In the back yard on the deck is a starry clear night looking up into the sky. This enhances the tranquility of marijuana. "I'm at Moms crib.onthemoon.com." I told T Grey [2:10:40 am/ 5-13-10].

Printed in the United States
By Bookmasters